THE Swamp

BY

Ed Hanson

THE BARCLAY FAMILY ADVENTURES

Development and Production: Laurel Associates, Inc.
Cover and Interior Art: Black Eagle Productions

 **SADDLEBACK**
PUBLISHING·INC.
Three Watson
Irvine, CA 92618-2767

Website: www.sdlback.com

ISBN 1-56254-558-2

Printed in the United States of America
08 07 06 05 04   9 8 7 6 5 4 3 2 1

CONTENTS

MEET THE BARCLAYS

Paul Barclay
A fun-loving father of three who takes his kids on his travels whenever he can.

Ann Barclay
The devoted mother who manages the homefront during Paul's many absences as an on-site construction engineer.

Jim Barclay
The eldest child, Jim is a talented athlete with his eye on a football scholarship at a major college.

Aaron Barclay
Three years younger than Jim, he's inquisitive, daring, and an absolute whiz in science class.

Pam Barclay
Adopted from Korea as a baby, Pam is a spunky middle-schooler who more than holds her own with her lively older brothers.

CHAPTER 1

Jack Sinclair

The sky that morning was gray and overcast—the kind of day that makes it hard to get out of bed. But more sleep wasn't an option for Jack Sinclair. All guests of the Florida prison system got up at 6 o'clock every morning.

After breakfast, Jack lined up with the other inmates to board the prison bus. In their orange jumpsuits, the men on the work detail all looked alike. The Florida prison system wasn't big on fashion.

Jack grabbed a seat by himself and stared out the window. He had just turned 21, and his life was a mess. And *why?* He hadn't done anything—nothing bad enough to deserve this.

He didn't claim to be an all-American boy. After his father had left, Jack had dropped out of school. He'd made a living by poaching animals in the Everglades.

Alligator hides brought $100 on the black market. A real big one might bring $150.

Jack also captured and sold exotic birds. All of this was illegal, of course. But if a guy knew the marsh, he could earn a living from it.

And Jack knew the marsh. He'd spent more than five years poaching wildlife there. Some of his friends had even started calling him "Swamper."

The trouble started late one night when he'd been out hunting 'gators. He'd stopped at an all-night supermarket for some bread. It was about 3 o'clock in the morning and the store was practically empty. A sleepy-looking clerk behind the checkout counter was reading the newspaper.

Jack headed to the back of the store. He picked up a loaf of bread and remembered he needed a quart of milk. As he turned around, he spotted Rip Poole. Rip wasn't a close friend, just a guy he knew.

"Hey, Rip. What are you doing here so late?" Jack asked.

Rip gave Jack a sly grin. "Same as you, I expect," he answered.

Jack carried his milk and bread to the checkout counter. Rip followed close behind.

Just as Jack was reaching for his wallet, Rip suddenly pulled a handgun from under his shirt! He pointed it at the clerk and barked, "Open the cash register, and make it fast!"

Jack was in shock. "Put that gun away, Rip! What do you think you're doing?"

"Shut up, Jack," was all Rip said.

The clerk stepped on a silent alarm button on the floor behind the counter. Knowing that it rang at the police station, he fumbled with the cash drawer to buy some time. "I can't get it open!" he said.

"Come on, Rip, you don't want to do this," Jack pleaded.

"I told you to shut up!" Rip hissed. Then he grabbed the clerk by the shirt and thrust the gun into his chest. "I mean it— get the money now!" he ordered.

As the cash drawer flew open, Rip jumped over the counter. He pushed the clerk aside and began to scoop up the bills. But just then, two police cars pulled up outside!

Jack and Rip saw the flashing lights at the same time. Rip yelled in outrage at the trembling clerk. "You signaled them!" Then he fired a shot into the man's chest.

With their guns drawn, two police officers came bursting through the front door. Jack raised his hands and cried out, "Don't shoot!"

Rip ran out a rear door. But two more officers were waiting for him in the alley. They ordered him to drop the gun.

Defiant to the end, Rip ignored them and ran down the alley. Then he turned and fired a shot at the pursuing police. They instantly returned fire—and Rip, just 22 years old, died in the alley outside the supermarket.

The police arrested Jack! He told them over and over that he wasn't with Rip, but they didn't believe him. The clerk couldn't help him. He was in a coma at the hospital and not expected to live. The only other person who could clear him was Rip. But Rip was dead.

Jack had no money. He couldn't afford his own lawyer. So the court appointed a pubic defender to represent him. Unfortunately, this appointed lawyer took little interest in the case and presented a half-hearted defense.

Jack hadn't shot anyone. He didn't even have a gun. Yet, here he was in a Florida prison, sentenced to 20 years. The court was convinced that Jack had aided in an armed robbery. In the eyes of the law, that made him as guilty as Rip. At the time of sentencing, Jack had just turned 19.

Two long years had passed. Now the sun was coming up, and Jack Sinclair was staring out the bus window. *I can't spend 18 more years like this,* he thought to himself. *I just can't!*

He'd plotted all sorts of escape plans.

But only one scheme made real sense to him. Jack had spent a lot of time in the Everglades, after all. If only he could get to the swamp, they'd never find him.

Someday, one of these work details will be near the Everglades, he thought to himself. *When that happens, I'm gone!* Just the thought of getting away brought a smile to his face.

CHAPTER 2

Arranging the Trip

Paul and Ann Barclay sat on the sand watching Aaron and Pam play in the surf. This was the third day of their vacation in Florida—and Paul was getting bored!

He turned to Ann and said, "Are you getting tired of sitting here on the beach every day?"

"Not really," Ann answered. "I find it peaceful and relaxing. But I know that you want to do something more exciting. What do you have in mind?"

"Well, I was thinking about chartering an airboat and touring the Everglades. It should be a lot of fun *and* educational for the kids," Paul answered.

"Do you know how to operate an airboat?" Ann asked.

"No," Paul answered. "We could hire a guide to take us. It's a popular thing for tourists to do."

"Sounds okay to me," Ann said. "Why don't you make the arrangements?"

After a few calls, Paul discovered that Bill Peterson's Airboat Tours had an opening for Thursday—the day after tomorrow. Paul settled on the price and asked Bill about lunch.

"No problem at all, Mr. Barclay. Lunch is included in the price. You and your family will have plenty to eat."

"Great," Paul said. "We'll see you at 8 o'clock on Thursday morning."

That evening over dinner, Paul told Aaron and Pam about Thursday's trip. They were both excited about seeing the Everglades, but Pam had some concerns about the airboat.

"Daddy," she said, "I read that airboats are so noisy they disturb the wildlife in the wetlands."

"Well, Buttons, they *are* noisy. Some people absolutely hate them. If you were canoeing or kayaking on a quiet waterway, you wouldn't like to listen to the racket of a motorized airboat speeding by.

"On the other hand, airboats offer a quick and easy way for people to see the swamp. And in an emergency, there's nothing that can get to the scene faster. Think about it: There's some good and bad in almost everything."

"Will we see alligators?" Aaron asked.

"I expect so, son. There sure are a lot of them in the park," Paul answered.

"We'll have to get up very early on Thursday," Paul continued. "It's an hour's drive to the marina, and I told them we'd be there at 8 o'clock."

"No problem," Ann said. "We'll get up at 6 o'clock, have a quick breakfast, and be on the road by 7 o'clock."

"Great!" Paul said. "That means I have only one more day to stare at the ocean."

CHAPTER 3

Escape

Jack Sinclair pulled himself out of bed to face another day. There were few surprises in prison. Every day was pretty much the same as the last. Today, however, would be very different. But Jack didn't know that yet.

Jack climbed aboard the prison bus with the rest of the work detail. He closed his eyes and tried to sleep. An hour later, he heard a guard's gruff voice. "Okay, everybody out!" the man ordered.

As Jack climbed down from the bus, he couldn't believe his eyes. *He knew exactly where he was.* Five years earlier, he had killed his first alligator less than 200 yards from where he now stood!

His mind was racing. They were right on the edge of the Everglades swamp. If he could slip into the marsh unseen, he was sure that he could escape. All he needed was a 10-minute head start while the guards weren't watching. The best time would be just before noon.

At the stroke of 12, the guards would blow a whistle. When the prisoners were back on the bus, box lunches would be handed out. Then, while the prisoners ate, the guards would take a head count. Before that, they wouldn't realize that anyone was missing.

As it got close to noon, Jack inched his way to the edge of the work detail. He waited for the whistle to blow. When the guard was distracted, he dropped to the ground in the bushes.

While everyone was lining up to board the bus, Jack headed straight into the swamp. He'd run about 200 yards when he could hear a commotion back on the road. He knew they'd discovered that someone was missing.

Jack remembered a small marina about six miles to the north. If he could get there, he might be able to steal an airboat. He turned toward Peterson's Airboat Tours and started running.

Back on the road, the guards had called for additional help. Soon a full search would be under way. Jack had to get rid of his orange jumpsuit! The next hour was critical to his escape.

He pushed on through the mangrove thickets. In some places the water was waist-deep. The air was humid, and he was soaked with perspiration.

There were many dangers in the Everglades, including alligators and several species of poisonous snakes. But Jack was more afraid of capture than anything the marsh could offer.

An hour later, Jack was staring through thick vegetation at a small house with a 20-foot dock. An airboat was tied to the dock. He watched Bill Peterson tinkering with the engine.

Then, Jack silently swam to the dock. He pulled himself from the water as Bill Peterson's back was turned.

The tour guide didn't hear Jack sneaking up behind him. Picking up a large crescent wrench from the dock, he slammed it down on Peterson's head.

Jack dragged the unconscious body to a back room in the house. Then he stripped off Bill's shirt and pants and put them on. He threw the prison jumpsuit in the trash. Next, he tied Bill's hands and feet and covered his mouth with duct tape.

On the desk in Bill's office, Jack found his leather appointment book. Right next to tomorrow's date was written: *8 A.M. day tour—the Barclay family.*

What a great cover! Jack thought to himself. *I'll pretend to be Bill Peterson and take these people on a tour of the park.*

He found a small handgun in a side drawer of the desk—and it was loaded. He put the gun in his pocket and settled down to wait for the next day.

CHAPTER 4

A Race Through the Swamp

It was 8:30 A.M. when Paul Barclay and his family pulled into the parking lot at Bill Peterson's marina. Paul locked the car and they all walked down to the dock.

Jack Sinclair eyed them nervously. He wasn't sure if Paul had met Bill before. He'd have to be ready for anything.

Paul walked up to Jack and said, "Good morning, Bill! I'm sorry we're late—we ran into a police roadblock."

Jack stayed calm. "Oh," he said. "What was that all about?"

"They said someone escaped from a prison work detail yesterday. There's a big search going on."

Jack's mind was racing. The only thing he could think about was getting deeper into the swamp. "Well, I hope they catch him. Now let's get started," he said.

After Paul introduced Ann and the kids, they took seats on the boat. Jack untied the mooring lines. Then he climbed up into the operator's seat and eased the boat away from the dock.

The powerful engine and the huge whirling airplane propeller made an awful racket, indeed. Pam covered her ears. Now she knew for sure why some people hated airboats. But as her father had told her, "There's usually some good and some bad in almost everything."

Jack headed into the marsh at a steady speed. In some places, it felt like they were skimming across dry land. But in fact, they were in shallow water covered with a thick bed of marsh grass.

The airboat flushed a number of birds from their nests. But it was traveling so fast there was no time to sightsee!

Ann leaned over and yelled to Paul above the engine noise. "Why is he going so darn fast? We could see a lot more if he'd slow down just a little bit!"

Paul agreed. He eased out of his seat and yelled to Jack. "Let's slow down so we can see more of the marsh!"

Jack turned to Paul. "We'll come to a great sightseeing area very shortly," he said. "I'll slow down then."

Paul wasn't pleased with the guide's response, but he accepted it without further thought.

For the next few hours, the airboat continued to roar through the Everglades. It was getting close to noon when Paul approached Jack again.

"Stop the boat, Bill," Paul insisted. "I want to talk with you."

Jack brought the boat to a stop and turned off the engine.

"We're getting hungry. Let's eat lunch now. After that, I want you to slow down so we can see the scenery," Paul said. "Where do you keep the lunches?"

"Unless you brought lunches with you there aren't any," Jack answered.

Paul had been uneasy, but now he was sure that something was wrong. "You aren't Bill Peterson, are you?" he asked.

"No, I'm not, "Jack answered as he pulled the small handgun from his pocket. "I don't want to hurt anyone, Mr. Barclay. Just do as you're told for the time being. In another hour you can have this boat, and I'll be gone."

Ann cried out without thinking. "Oh, no, Paul!" she said. "He must be the convict who escaped yesterday!"

Jack sneered at her. "You're right, lady. Now *sit down*! We only have a few more miles to go."

When Jack started up the engine, Paul whispered to Ann. "I'm going to jump him. When I do, you'll have to take over the controls. Just try to stop the boat."

Ann's face went pale. "Please don't, Paul. I'm scared," she whispered.

"So am I, honey. But we have to do something to stop this criminal!"

Taking a deep breath, Paul leaped

from his seat and pulled Jack down onto the deck. As the two men struggled, the airboat went out of control. When it veered to the left, Ann tried to move forward to the driver's seat. But she lost her balance and was thrown into the water.

Seconds later, the boat struck the stump of a cypress tree and flipped over. Along with Paul and Jack, Pam was thrown free and landed in the water. The thick layers of marsh grass saved them from serious injury.

The airboat ended up a twisted hulk in four feet of water. The Barclays could see chunks of bent metal poking out of the water. The boat was a total wreck!

Pam and her mother waded to a dry mangrove thicket. Although shaken up by the experience, neither was badly hurt. Paul dragged Jack Sinclair to the mangrove thicket by the scruff of his neck. He knew that the escaped prisoner was no longer a threat. Paul had seen him lose his gun in the struggle.

"Where's Aaron?" Pam cried out.

"Aaron! *Aaron!*" Paul yelled.

"Over here, Dad!" Aaron yelled back. "I'm stuck here in the boat!"

They all waded back into the water and made their way toward the mangled airboat. Sure enough, Aaron was trapped in the twisted wreckage. Luckily, he was unhurt. But Paul estimated that it would take several hours to free him.

CHAPTER 5

The Rescue

Sitting on the edge of the mangrove thicket, Jack thought about taking off. The Barclays were trying to free their son in the wreckage. They weren't watching him.

But there was a new danger that only his keen eye detected. He tried to shake it off. *Come on, Jack, get moving,* he said to himself. *That kid isn't your responsibility.*

But somehow he was frozen. In his heart he knew it was his fault that Aaron was trapped in the wreck. *I just can't leave the kid to die here in front of his parents,* he thought.

Jack shrugged and waded into the water. When he reached the boat, he said, "Mr. Barclay?"

Paul turned. "What are *you* still doing here?" he asked angrily.

Jack looked ashamed. "I figure all of this is my fault. I want to help you get your son free," he answered in a soft voice.

Paul looked at him scornfully. "I don't need your help!" he snapped.

"Oh, yes, you do. There's something you don't know. We're in a tidal section of the swamp near the ocean. Right now, the tide is coming in. In another 30 minutes, your boy will be underwater."

Paul was stunned. He looked around and realized that Jack was right. Now Paul noticed the high water marks on all the surrounding trees. At high tide, Aaron would be drowned!

"I don't think we can free him in 30 minutes," Paul said.

"Maybe not. But the two of us will have a better chance," Jack answered.

For the next 20 minutes, Paul and Jack struggled with the twisted metal. Ann felt completely helpless as she watched the rising water threaten to engulf her son.

"It's no use! We'll never get him out in time!" Paul cried out in despair.

Aaron was fighting to keep his nose

and mouth above the water. After a few more breaths of air, the rising tide would cover him!

Jack turned to Paul. "Do you have a knife?" he asked.

"Yes. Why?"

"Just give it to me," Jack demanded.

Paul was desperate. He handed his pocket knife to the prisoner.

Jack swam to the back of the boat and disappeared underwater. Seconds later he popped to the surface, holding an 18-inch piece of tubing he'd cut from the engine. He quickly placed one end of the tube in Aaron's mouth.

"You'll have to breathe through this tube until we can get you free," he said. "Relax, kid. You can do it."

Paul was amazed. He would have never thought of a breathing tube!

"Mrs. Barclay," Jack continued, "could you hold the other end of this tube so it stays out of the water?"

Ann took the tube in one hand and

held Aaron's hand with the other.

Again Paul and Jack attacked the crumpled wreckage. Some of the pieces were too thick to bend. Jack looked over at Paul's grim face.

"There was a tool box on the boat," he said. "I think I saw a hacksaw in it. I'm going to see if I can find it."

For the first time, Paul noticed how young Jack was. "What's your real name, anyway?" he asked.

"It's Jack—Jack Sinclair. And I'm sure sorry for all this trouble."

Paul squeezed his arm. "Well, Jack, you're sure making up for it now."

It took Jack five dives to find the toolbox. Then he attacked the largest piece of metal with the hacksaw. Progress was slow, but the opening was finally large enough for Aaron to slip through.

As Aaron's head bobbed up out of the water, he spit out the tube and took in a big gulp of air. Then they all waded to the dry mangrove thicket.

"Tell me, Jack," Paul asked. "What made you change your mind? Why did you decide to stay and help us?"

"I don't really know. I guess I didn't want to be responsible for Aaron's death."

As they all rested, Jack told them the story of the supermarket robbery.

"No one would believe I wasn't part of the robbery. I tried to get Rip to stop—but he wouldn't listen to me."

Paul and Ann had the same thought: *This young man wasn't really a bad guy.*

"My father left us when I was 13," Jack went on. "I haven't seen him since. I quit school at 15, but I couldn't find work. So I started poaching in the Everglades. I earned enough to keep myself in food and clothes—and even to help my mom a little! Everything was okay until I ran into Rip in that supermarket."

CHAPTER 6

No More Running

"You know," Jack said, "we're only about four or five miles from the edge of the marsh. If we leave now, we can get out of here before dark."

"What are you going to do then, Jack?" Paul asked.

"Just keep on running, I guess," Jack answered. "If I give myself up, they'll send me right back to prison."

"Well, Jack, I guess that's true," Paul said quietly. "But what if we could get your case reopened? A better attorney might be able to convince the court that your 20-year sentence was unfair. There are no guarantees, of course—but wouldn't it be worth a try?"

"But I don't have any money to hire a good lawyer," Jack said sadly. "And even if I did, I don't know anyone. And on top of that, I can't really *prove* that I wasn't with

Rip! Who's going to believe me?"

"*I* believe you," Paul answered. "And I have a good friend in Fort Lauderdale who's a criminal lawyer. I'd be willing to talk with him about your case."

As Jack thought about Paul's offer, he saw Pam approaching a mound of dirt near the water's edge.

"Pam, get away from there!" he screamed. In a flash he grabbed her by the arm and pulled her away from the dirt pile.

They all watched in horror as a huge alligator suddenly charged from thick cover! It stopped when it saw Jack and Pam racing away from the pile.

"That mound of dirt is where that alligator laid her eggs," Jack explained. "She's very protective of it."

Everyone moved a safe distance away. Then they watched the 'gator settle down to protect her nest.

"I'm glad you're with us, Jack," Ann said. "Here in the swamp, you're a pretty valuable guy to have around!"

"Well, I've spent a lot of time out here. I've learned to recognize things."

They continued wading through the marsh. "We'll be back to civilization soon," Paul said. "Have you made up your mind, Jack? What's it going to be?"

"Do you *really* think there's a chance to get my case reviewed?" Jack asked.

"There's always a chance, Jack. And any chance is better than no chance. Living as a fugitive, you'll always be looking over your shoulder to see who's coming."

The Barclays and the prisoner reached a paved road at about 5 o'clock.

"There's a little restaurant not far from here," Jack said. "You must be hungry—I know I am. I haven't eaten since yesterday morning. But, Mr. Barclay, I don't have any money."

"Don't worry. I think I can afford a few burgers," Paul said.

Everyone had two burgers except Jack and Aaron. They had three!

Halfway through the meal, Jack said,

"I've been thinking about what you said, Mr. Barclay. I think I will give myself up. Would you call the authorities for me?"

"Sure, Jack. I can do that. But let's finish these burgers first. It may be a while before you eat anything this good again!"

About 20 minutes later, Paul placed a call from the restaurant. In no time, the state police arrived. After placing Jack in custody, they arranged transportation back to the marina for the Barclays.

They all felt exhausted as they drove back to their hotel. "Well, this was a typical day on a Paul Barclay trip," Ann said. "We were taken prisoner by an escaped convict and then rushed through the Everglades in a speeding airboat.

"After that, we were thrown into the water when the boat went out of control and crashed. And poor Aaron came close to drowning when he got trapped in the wreckage. Let's see, kids—did I forget anything?"

"How about me being chased by a

32

mother alligator who was protecting her nest?" Pam added.

"Oh, yes," Ann sighed. "How could I forget a small detail like that? Admit it, Paul. It's really a wonder that anyone in this family is still alive!"

Paul winked at her. "Oh, don't be so negative," he said. "It's the excitement that makes these trips so much fun. Besides— eventually you'll look back on today as a great memory!"

Aaron looked at his mother. "I agree with *you*, Mom. I'm afraid that Dad is a little crazy."

The bantering continued until they reached Miami.

CHAPTER 7

Laying Plans

The next morning Paul got up early to call his friend, Walt Coles. Walt had built up a fine law practice in southern Florida. Paul was sure that he could help Jack.

The last time he'd seen Walt was a year ago. That was when Paul had visited Florida with his son, Jim. On a diving trip, a giant squid attacked them. Walt always teased Jim that every time he told the squid story, the creature got bigger.

"Paul! How are you doing?" Walt said when he heard his friend's voice.

"I'm doing fine, old buddy. Is there any chance you can break away for an hour or so today?"

"Well, I'm in court all morning, but I could probably meet you for lunch," Walt answered.

They agreed on a restaurant, and Paul said, "I'll see you at noon."

Walt had already been seated in a corner booth when Paul arrived. The old friends shook hands.

"Tell me something, Paul. How big is that squid when Jim tells that story now?"

Paul laughed. "Let's see. The last time I heard it, the squid was as big as a two-story house."

Walt laughed. "Jim's a great kid! Tell him I asked about him," he said.

"I sure will, Walt. But I wanted to talk to you about another young man."

Then Paul told Jack Sinclair's story. When he was finished, Walt said, "Let me get this straight. You want to help this guy after he kidnapped your whole family and almost got you killed?"

"He saved Aaron's life, Walt."

"Sure—but don't forget that he put Aaron in danger in the first place!"

"I know that. But he could have run— and he didn't," Paul answered.

"And another thing, old friend. You have only his word that he wasn't in on the robbery. He could have been, you know. What if he's lying?"

"Look, Walt, I know that everything you say is true. But I believe him, and I want to help him. Do you think you can get his case reopened?"

"Have you thought about what a case like this will cost?" Walt asked.

"No, not really. Why?"

"I won't charge you for my time," Walt continued, "but there will be plenty of other expenses. Why, I figure that you're probably looking at a minimum of $8,000 to $10,000."

Paul looked shocked. But then he thought for a moment.

"Isn't a young man's life worth that much?" he asked.

"I guess it is," Walt said thoughtfully. "I guess it is.

"Okay, I'll look into the case and see what I can find out. I'll do my best to keep your costs down, and I'll get back to you when I have something."

"Thanks, Walt," Paul said warmly. "I knew I could count on you!"

"Hey, I'm not so sure that I'm doing you a favor," Walt said. "But if you're sure it's what you want—"

"I'm sure, Walt. That's what I want," Paul answered.

CHAPTER 8

New Evidence

Almost a month had gone by since the Barclay family had returned from Florida. Paul hadn't talked with Jack in weeks, and he wondered how he was doing.

Paul also wondered how Walt was doing. He was tempted to call him. But he knew that Walt would report in when he had something to tell him.

Lost in thought, Paul almost didn't hear the phone ring. He picked up the receiver and said, "Hello."

"Paul, it's Walt. I've some good news."

"Gee, I was just thinking about you. I've been wondering what was going on," Paul answered.

"Well, Paul, I talked with the clerk who was in the store at the time of the robbery. He's fully recovered now. He told me Jack came in a few minutes after Rip Poole did. He also said that Jack didn't have a gun. In fact, he doesn't think Jack was involved."

"That's *great!*" Paul said.

"But there's more, Paul. There was another customer in the store that night."

"You're kidding," Paul answered.

"No, I'm not. An elderly lady saw everything. When she saw Rip pull out a gun, she hid behind a display. I talked with the woman yesterday. She's willing to testify that Jack actually tried to stop the robbery."

Paul cried out, "That's *wonderful!*"

"With this new evidence, we have a good chance to get Jack's case reopened," Walt added.

"Why didn't this information come out at the first trial?" Paul asked.

"That's hard to say. It could be that the public defender had too many cases to spend much time on Jack's. Or maybe it was just sloppy legal work. It happens."

"Have you told Jack the good news yet?" Paul asked.

"No, I thought I'd let you do that."

"I can't thank you enough, my friend. I'll call him today," Paul said.

"Good. I'll get to work on the appeal. Nothing will happen overnight. The wheels of justice move slowly, you know. But I'll keep you informed. And, Paul—there's just one more thing."

"What's that?"

"Bill Peterson is still out an airboat. If Jack could replace the airboat he stole, it would help his appeal."

"Gosh," Paul said. "I'd forgotten all about that. Let me work on it."

Paul put the phone down and thought about what Walt had just told him. He was already doing a lot to help Jack. Paying for an expensive airboat would be going too far. Besides, he had Ann and their own three children to provide for.

Later that day, Paul called Jack. He told him about the new witness. Jack was surprised. He couldn't stop thanking Paul for his help.

"But there's one more problem you

need to take care of, Jack," Paul said.

"What's that?" Jack asked.

"You still owe Bill Peterson for the airboat you took. That's a *lot* of money. I'm willing to replace it on one condition."

Jack was stunned. "Anything you say, Mr. Barclay!" he answered eagerly.

"The condition is this: When you're out of prison and get a job, you pay me back in monthly installments."

"Yes, sir. In fact, I'll find *two* jobs and repay every nickel as soon as possible."

"Okay, Jack, we have a deal. Stay out of trouble and write me from time to time."

"I sure will, Mr. Barclay. And thanks again for everything."

Paul didn't think Ann would object to his offer. She'd taken a real liking to Jack. But marriage is a partnership—the money he was spending was her money, too.

CHAPTER 9

A Second Trial

Two months later, Judge Vandecourt opened hearings on Jack Sinclair's case. The proceedings were in Miami.

Paul and Ann were on hand to offer Jack their support. He was wearing a prison uniform when he was led into the courtroom.

Walt Cole presented a strong case. He stated that Jack had not entered the store with Rip Poole. Jack had no plans to rob the market, Walt explained. He was there only to buy milk and bread. The store clerk and another customer were now ready to testify that Jack had no part in the robbery.

Judge Vandecourt was convinced. The evidence was overwhelming.

After the hearing, Paul grabbed Jack by the arm. "Keep your chin up, Jack. You'll be free soon!"

Then the guards led him away. Even

though he was going back to prison, Jack felt great. For almost the first time in his life, he didn't feel alone.

The second trial ended quickly. The evidence proved that Jack had been wrongly convicted. The surprise witness, Clara Perkins, called Jack "that young man who tried his best to stop the robbery."

The district attorney questioned Mrs. Perkins closely. He demanded to know why she was in the market so late and why she hadn't testified earlier.

She calmly explained that she liked shopping when she had the store to herself and could take her time. As to why she hadn't testified at the first trial, she simply said, "I was never asked."

Even Bill Peterson had become one of Jack's supporters. After Paul replaced his airboat, his only gripe was the knock on the head that Jack had given him. But he forgave him for that.

"If I'd been sent up for a crime I didn't commit, I'd try to escape, too," Bill said.

The final blow to the state's case was the store clerk's testimony. Fully recovered from the gunshot wound, he stated that Jack had not entered the store with Poole.

"In my opinion, he had nothing to do with the robbery," he stated.

In less than an hour, the jury returned with a *not guilty* verdict. Jack Sinclair was now a free man!

That evening, Paul and Ann took Jack out to dinner. "So what are you going to do now?" Paul asked.

"First I need a job to pay my way," Jack answered. "And I also want to get my high school diploma."

"That's a very good idea," Ann said.

"Yeah, I realize now that dropping out of school was stupid," Jack added.

"I've got a number of friends in the construction industry," Paul said. "I can get you a job with a good company—if you're willing to work hard."

"Oh, Mr. Barclay!" Jack grinned. "I'd really appreciate that. And don't worry about whether or not I'll work hard. Why, I'll be the best worker they ever saw!"

"Okay, Jack, I'll get to work on it. And I think that it's about time you started calling us Paul and Ann. This 'Mr. and Mrs.' stuff sounds too formal."

"Whatever you say, Mr. Barclay—I mean Paul," Jack answered.

The next month saw a lot of changes in Jack Sinclair's life. Paul had gotten him a job in construction. Although Jack was only a laborer, he took all the overtime work he could get.

He brought home a good salary and faithfully sent Paul a monthly payment. Jack had also signed up for night courses, and was working toward getting his high school diploma.

After two and a half years behind bars, life was suddenly good again.

CHAPTER 10

The Invitation

Now it was early December. A light snow was falling in Rockdale as Paul and Ann were enjoying a quiet Saturday morning. Jim was away at college, and Aaron and Pam had gone off somewhere with friends.

Between sips of coffee, Ann looked at Paul and smiled. "I have an idea. What would you say to inviting Jack to spend Christmas with us?"

"I think that's a *great* idea!" Paul said enthusiastically. "He's been working six days a week since his release. A little vacation would be good for him."

"I agree. And I don't think he's ever seen snow," Ann added.

"Well, he certainly never saw any in southern Florida!"

Early the next morning, Paul placed a telephone call. "Hi, Jack," Paul said.

"How's everything going with you?"

Jack filled Paul in on what had happened since they'd last talked. When he finished, Paul asked him if he'd like to visit them over Christmas.

Jack was stunned. "I'd really love that!" he answered. "I've never been out of Florida, you know."

"That's great, Jack. We'll look forward to seeing you again. Make your plane reservations. Then call me with your flight number and arrival time, and I'll meet you at the airport," Paul offered.

That evening, Ann told Aaron and Pam that Jack would be visiting them over the holidays.

"Oh, that's cool!" Pam said. "I like Jack, and I feel so bad that he wasted two years of his life in prison."

"Well, you *ought* to like him," Aaron chimed in. "If it wasn't for Jack, you'd have been alligator food!"

Ignoring her brother's remark, Pam asked, "How in the world could the court ever make such an awful mistake?"

"Well, Buttons," Paul said, "lots of things that happen in life aren't what they seem to be. That was the situation in Jack's case. He was in the wrong place at the wrong time—so he *appeared* to be guilty."

"But it's just not fair," Pam insisted.

"Let me give you kids an example," Paul continued. "Suppose I offer you a job for one month—30 days. And suppose I offered to pay you for your work in one of two different ways. You get to pick which way you want to be paid."

"All right," Aaron answered, "and what are our choices?"

"Your first choice," Paul said, "is to be paid $50,000 for the month."

"Wow!" Pam squealed. "That's a whole lot of money."

"It sure is, Buttons. It's more than most people make by working hard for a whole year," Paul went on.

"Your second choice is this: I pay you one penny for your first day's work and double that amount each day after that. In other words, you'd get one cent for day one, two cents for day two, four cents for day three, and so on. What's your choice? Which way do you want to be paid?"

Aaron and Pam thought about it for a while. Aaron answered first. "That's not a very tough decision, Dad. Anyone would take the $50,000. It would be dumb not to."

"Do you agree, Pam?" Paul asked.

"Of course I do!" she laughed.

Paul smiled and said, "Well, you'd be making a terrible mistake. If you took the other plan, you'd have more than five million dollars that month."

Aaron and Pam stared at each other. "No way!" they cried out in unison.

Paul laughed. "Why don't you get a pencil and paper and work it out?"

Fifteen minutes later, Aaron and Pam came back to their dad.

"You're right!" they shouted. "We still can hardly believe it—but we worked it out on paper and it's true."

"Now do you see what I mean, kids? Things aren't always what they seem to be," Paul said with a chuckle.

CHAPTER 11

The Crash

On December 21, Paul sat in Logan Airport, waiting for Jack's flight from Florida. He reflected on that fateful day when he'd first met Jack at the airboat pier. He thought about the wild ride through the Everglades, the airboat crash, and the desperate struggle to save Aaron from drowning.

After all that, it would have been easy to walk away from Jack. But Paul was glad that he hadn't. He felt good about helping the unfortunate young man pull his life together. And he was proud that Jack was working so hard to repay him.

Then the loudspeaker announced the arrival of flight 175 from Miami. Paul snapped out of his daydream. Moments later, Jack walked into the terminal, carrying a large duffel bag. He looked older and much more confident than he had when Paul had first met him.

"Hi, Jack! Welcome to Boston," Paul said as he shook Jack's hand.

Jack was grinning from ear to ear. "Hi, Mr. Barclay. It's great to see you."

"Hey, it's *Paul*—remember?"

"Oh, yeah," Jack responded. "I'll get it right in time."

When they arrived back in Rockdale, the rest of the family was waiting to greet their guest. The kids hadn't seen him in over a year. They wanted to hear about everything he'd been doing. The rest of the day was spent getting caught up on each other's activities.

The next day, Aaron and Pam took Jack ice skating. Since he'd never been on skates before, Jack spent a lot of time picking himself up from the ice. Aaron and Pam laughed as Jack struggled to keep his balance, only to fall again.

"Keep trying, Jack!" Pam shouted. "You'll get the hang of it."

"By the time I get the hang of it, I'll be

too sore to walk," Jack yelled back.

At dinner that evening, Ann asked Jack about his day.

"It was okay, I guess—except for Aaron and Pam trying to *kill* me," he teased.

"Oh, Jack—you did great for your first time on skates," Pam laughed. "In another couple of days, you'll skate like a pro."

"That's what you think, little girl," Jack answered. "My skating days are over. How about a nice quiet movie tomorrow?"

Everyone laughed except Pam. She rolled her eyes and said, "*Wimp.*"

When dinner was over, Pam kissed her father on the cheek and asked him to drive her to the mall.

Ann observed the scene from across the room. She chuckled to herself. When had Pam learned to get her way by being coy and affectionate with her father?

"Please, Daddy! There are a couple of last-minute presents I need to find before Christmas."

"I'll take her if you'd rather stay here,"

Jack volunteered. "I need to buy a few things, too."

"Thanks, Jack," Paul answered. "I don't feel much like going out tonight. The car keys are on the table in the hall."

Grabbing their coats, Pam and Jack headed out the door. The slight drizzle coming down had left a light coating of ice all over the car. Before starting the engine, Jack got out the scraper and cleaned the windshield.

"Now, Jack, I don't want you following me around the mall," Pam said laughingly. "Know why? Because one of the things I'm looking for is a present for *you!*"

"Well," Jack answered, "I'm certainly not going to let you wander around the mall at night alone. Besides, just being here is my present!"

Pam looked at Jack with wide eyes. "After you give me a gift, how would I feel if I didn't have one for you?"

"What makes you think I have a gift for you?" Jack asked with a smile.

Pam smirked. "Because, Jack Sinclair, when I was looking for my snowshoes, I happened to see some presents in the corner of your closet. And one of them had my name on it."

"You're a little sneak, do you know that?" Jack said as he reached over and playfully mussed her hair.

"You may as well tell me now. What did you get me, Jack?" Pam asked.

"None of your business," Jack said, trying to change the subject. "How far away is this mall, anyway?"

"Just a few more miles. Take a right at the traffic light that's coming up."

As Jack approached the intersection, the light turned green. He flipped on his turn signal and started to make the turn.

Suddenly, out of nowhere, a pickup truck skidded through the red light! It slammed into the driver's side of the Barclays' car. The impact drove the car up over the sidewalk and slammed it into a big oak tree. Glass was everywhere, and

Pam's door was gaping open! Only her seat belt prevented her from being thrown from the car.

Pam was dazed for several seconds. What had happened? Her brain gradually began to function. *We've been in an accident,* she thought to herself. She looked over at Jack.

"Jack, Jack! Are you okay?"

There was no answer. In the darkness all Pam could see was a limp figure slumped over the steering wheel. How could she get him out of the car?

Pam unlatched her seat belt and reached over to release Jack's. Then she grabbed his shoulders and tried to pull him over to the passenger's side. He was heavy! It took all her strength, but finally she moved him away from the steering wheel. After pulling him from the car, she dragged his limp body 20 feet from the wreckage.

Pam could see that Jack's lower left leg was badly injured. Blood was pouring out of a long gash below his knee. She knew she had to do something to stop the bleeding. Taking the belt from her jeans, she secured it tightly around his left thigh.

By now, a crowd was starting to gather. People seemed to be coming from every direction. Someone put a blanket around her shoulders. When she heard sirens blaring in the distance, Pam dropped to her knees and burst into tears.

CHAPTER 12

The Recovery

Pam opened her eyes and saw her mother and father looking down at her. A quick look around the room told her that she was in the hospital.

"Hi there, Buttons," Paul said as he gently squeezed her hand.

"What happened?" Pam asked.

"Don't you remember, honey? You were in a bad accident," Ann answered.

"What about Jack? Is he all right?"

A doctor came into the room just then. Hearing Pam's question, he said, "Thanks to you, he's going to live. That belt you tightened around his leg slowed down the bleeding. Without it, I'm not sure we could have saved him."

"And what about *you*, young lady?" the doctor went on. "How are you feeling?"

"Okay, I guess," Pam answered.

"You've had quite a shock, but nothing

appears to be broken. I see no reason why you can't go home. Why don't you get dressed while I talk with your parents for a moment?"

Ann and Paul joined the doctor in the hallway. "We're glad to report that your friend, Jack, is going to live," the doctor said. "But there's a problem."

Paul put his arm around Ann. "What's that?" he asked.

"The pickup truck that smashed into your car completely crushed Jack's left foot. I'm afraid we can't save it."

"Oh, no!" Paul gasped.

"Believe me, Mr. Barclay, we did everything we could," the doctor went on. "But the damage was just too severe."

"Does Jack know yet?" Paul asked.

"No. I thought you folks might want to tell him," the doctor explained.

Ann returned to be with Pam. Paul's heart was heavy as he walked toward Jack's room. He dreaded telling him the bad news. He was trying to think of an easier way, but there simply wasn't one.

"Hi, Jack, how are you feeling?" Paul asked softly.

"Hi, Paul," Jack answered in a groggy voice. "I'm real sorry about the car."

"Forget about the car, Jack. It wasn't your fault. The important thing is that you and Pam are alive."

"How's Pam? The doctor says that I might have died if it weren't for her. I guess I owe her my life."

"Hey," Paul said. "You would have done the same for her. Besides—she thinks of you as another brother. So I guess you could say that it's all in the family.

"Listen, Jack. There's something I have to tell you now—and I don't know of any easy way to do it."

Fighting back tears, Paul put his hand on Jack's shoulder. "The accident crushed your left foot, Jack. It's so badly damaged that the doctors can't save it."

The room was silent as Jack stared into space. Finally, he turned to Paul and said,

"You know, I suspected the news was worse than the doctors were telling me. I just had this funny feeling."

"Look, Jack, you must feel terrible right now. This is horrible news. But you're young and strong and have 100 percent of our support! Four or five months from now—with an artificial foot—you'll be doing everything you ever did."

Jack's pale face looked doubtful. "Do you really think so, Paul?" he asked.

"I *know* so! Medical science has made tremendous progress in prosthetics. It's *unbelievable*, in fact. Do you know that a young man ran a marathon last year after losing part of his leg?"

Jack wiped the tears from his cheeks. "No, I didn't know that," he answered.

"Why don't you stay up here with us while you're recuperating, Jack? In a few months you'll be comfortable with your new foot. Then you can go back to Florida if you want. But we'd really like for you to move north for good. Getting a job is no problem—I have lots of contacts in the construction industry. But that's not a decision that you need to make now. It's just something to think about."

*   *   *

Five months later it was hard to tell that Jack had any disability at all. Not only did he walk without a limp, he even played basketball at the YMCA!

As Paul had suggested, Jack had moved north to be near the Barclays. His attitude had been so positive that the doctors had asked him to help other patients.

So now Jack was volunteering his time, helping other accident victims cope with similar losses. Jack Sinclair had come a long, long way from his prison cell.

COMPREHENSION QUESTIONS

Who and Where?

1. Who once made a living poaching in a swamp?

2. In what state are the Everglades located?

3. Who robbed the all-night supermarket?

4. After his escape, who did Jack pretend to be?

5. Who was the first to guess that Jack was the escaped criminal?

6. Who almost drowned in the sinking airboat?

7. Who was Paul's attorney friend in Fort Lauderdale?

8. Who bought Bill Peterson a new airboat?

Remembering Details

1. How long was Jack's prison sentence?

2. What three things did Jack do to Bill Peterson?

3. What animal tried to protect the eggs she'd laid in a dirt mound?

4. What was the verdict at Jack's second trial?

5. How did Jack lose his left foot?

6. After his recovery, what sport did Jack learn to play?

7. Why did Jack move from Florida to the Northeast?